Happy Birthday, Bob!

A Snowman named just Bob

Illustrated by
Karen Hillard Good

Written by
Mark Kimball Moulton

ideals children's books.
Nashville, Tennessee

ISBN 978-0-8249-5596-0

Published by Ideals Children's Books
An imprint of Ideals Publications
A Guideposts Company
Nashville, Tennessee
www.idealsbooks.com

Library of Congress CIP data on file

Printed and bound in China

10 9 8 7 6 5 4 3 2 1

For our treasured families and friends,
the moon, the stars, tiny little snowflakes,
carrots... each other...

...and all the innocent bystanders
who get caught up in the magic.

-Karen and Mark

Gladly presented to:

On this day:

From:

It was late
that one Thanksgiving
when Bob first
came to me . . .
a joyful day
of food and fun,
with friends
and family.

We'd feasted well, as I recall,

on Mother's fine-cooked fare,

then settled down to rest a while and nap without a care.

No one knew what was to be, as daylight grew quite dim,

that soon our lives would change so much,

simply because of him.

The **weatherman** reported that no **snow** was due that night,
but as we slept, the **clouds** rolled in, obscuring all the **light**.
And though that weatherman had tried, he never could have said,
just what was forming in the **sky**, directly overhead!

The **Moon** grew bright,
then **disappeared**,
then broke into a **laugh**.
The **stars** began to dance a **jig**,
the **clouds** just split in half.

In retrospect I do believe

that **magic** came that night—

no ordinary **storm**, you see,

could stir up such a **sight**.

The sky began to whip around,
then settled on its way.

The wind skipped lightly through the trees,
inviting me to play.

And late that eve,

there fell the first

exquisite,

tiny

flake—

followed by **another**
and still others in its wake!

And this is when, I dare to say,
that Bob first came to be,

as peace fell lightly
like a robe
o'er every hill
and tree.

He fell upon my **windowsill**.
He landed in my **hair**.
He frosted all my neighbors' homes
and blew throughout the **air**.

Just when it seemed
the **storm** might pass,
or at least be quite mild,
the **Moon** came out and gave a wink
and then stood back and **smiled**.

'Twas like he knew the answer
to a real-life **mystery**—
a delightful understanding that
would soon be clear to me.

The snow took on an eerie cast—
first pink, then blue,
then gold.
Then anxious little whirlwinds
leaped around my feet, so bold!

Suddenly, I heard Bob whisper—
his voice was soft and kind.
He asked me if I'd help him then,
if I was so inclined,

to gather up those many flakes
and roll them in a ball,
till he could be, and be with me,
in shape and form and all.

"But Bob," I cried, "I just don't know where you are in all of this!
'Cause all of you is everywhere throughout this snowy-ness!
You're scattered over everything! How do you recommend
that I gather all your goodness up and make a perfect friend?"

'Twas then Bob shared a **secret**,
and I knew just what to do,
for he **whispered** these few words to me
that I now share with you—

"Friendship is a simple thing~
The clue is just to start,
As long as it is built on trust~
And love from in your heart."

I ran into my mother's house
to wake those sleepy folk.
I bid them come and help me
to roll and pat and poke
and build that grand ol' snowman
and do a right good job,
to bring to life
my special friend,
my snowman named
just "Bob."

We laughed and sang
and ran about
as Bob began to be.
We gathered up
what we would need—
everything was free!

Some coal for eyes,
a carrot nose,
some sticks,
a scarf,
a hat—
a smile so wide
it warmed your heart,
a coat,
and that was that.

Perhaps you may think so far that **magic** ruled that day,
but **so far** will seem like **nothing** compared to what was on its way!

For this is when our new friend, Bob, decided to awake.

He opened up his **twinkling eyes**;

his belly, it did shake.

His **voice**, I do remember,
was something of a **dream**.
His **countenance**, so pleasing—
unearthly, it did seem.

And though you might
be doubtful—
a **talking friend**
made out of **snow**?
This is what we heard from Bob—
he wanted us to know:

"You've given me my **eyes**
so I might see and blink,
a **mouth**, a **hat**, a **carrot** nose
so I might speak and think.

"The **scarf**, indeed, is cozy;
it's sure to keep me warm.
And thank you all for giving me
such a shapely **form**!

"I hope it **snows** aplenty
so I might stay and share
in all your loving **friendship**,
your thoughtful, tender **care**.

"But when it **warms** or if in spring,
you miss that I'm not near,
put a **sign** in your front yard
that reads just:

"Bob was here.""

Well, that was it . . .
'twas all Bob said
that dreamy,
starry night.

He'd said his piece, he closed his eyes,
yet everything seemed right.